W9-CBI-318

DISCARD

First Flight

Westville Public Library
153 Main, P O Box 789
Westville, IN 46391-0789

First Flight

by David McPhail

Little, Brown and Company
Boston   Toronto   London

for Brecon

and

for Melanie

(After all, it was her idea!)

Copyright © 1987 by David McPhail

All rights reserved. No part of this book may be reproduced in any form or by any
electronic or mechanical means, including information storage and retrieval system
without permission in writing from the publisher, except by a reviewer who may
quote brief passages in a review.

First Edition

Library of Congress Cataloging-in-Publication Data

McPhail, David M.
   First flight.

   Summary: A naughty teddy bear, in contrast with his well-behaved owner,
ignores all the rules and disrupts their first airplane trip.
ISBN 0-316-56323-4 (hc)
ISBN 0-316-56332-3 (pb)
   [1. Airplanes—Fiction. 2. Flight—Fiction.
3. Teddy bears—Fiction] I. Title.
PZ7.M2427Fg 1986   [F.]   86-28804

HC: 10 9 8 7 6 5 4
PB: 10 9 8 7 6 5 4 3 2

Published simultaneously in Canada
by Little, Brown & Company (Canada) Limited

Printed in the United States of America

I'm going to visit my grandma. I'm going to fly.
It will be my first flight.

My mother and father drive me to the airport.

I get my ticket…

find my gate…

and go through security.

While I'm waiting,
I watch them get my plane ready.

11

When my number is called, I get on the plane.

I find my seat

and put away my suitcase.

I buckle my seat belt and listen to the safety rules.

I sit back and relax while the plane takes off.

I look out the window.

The world below is getting smaller. I think I see my house.

In a little while lunch is served.

After lunch there's a movie.

It's kind of sad ... but it has a happy ending.

When the movie is over, I go to the bathroom.

The plane begins to bounce. The captain asks us to take our seats.

We are flying through a storm. The plane bounces a lot!

The captain calls it "turbulence."

When the plane stops bouncing, I read my book.

I'm tired. I take a nap.

I wake up when I hear something go "bump."
It is the landing gear. We are coming in for a landing!

I check my seat belt. Almost before I know it, we are on the ground.

When we arrive at the gate, I undo my seat belt and collect my things.

As I'm getting off the plane,
the captain stops me.

He says I was a good passenger.
He gives me some wings just like his.

My grandmother is waiting for me.

"How was your first flight?" she asks.

"Wonderful!" I say, and I tell her all about it.

DISCARD

E
MCP

McPhail, David M.

First flight.

$14.45

DATE		
FEB. 1 6 1995		
MAR. 6 1995		
JUL 1 3 1995		
FEB 28 1996		
APR. 8 1996		
OCT. 5 1996		
FE 10 '97		
JE 05 '97		
SE 14 '99		
MAR 04 2004		

Westville Public Library
153 Main P O Box 789
Westville, IN 46391-0739

BAKER & TAYLOR